CHANDELIERS

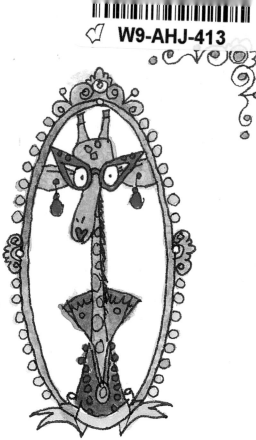

MRS. DAPHNE CHANDELIER is happy to be back on the stage at long last. Ten months ago, she absentmindedly boarded a hot-air balloon and sailed around the world twice. While in midair, she entertained seagulls and other birds with her famous songs "I Never Go Anywhere Without a Parasol" and "My Head Is in the Clouds."

GRANDDADDY CHANDELIER made his theatrical debut in the play *Things Are Looking Up* when he was only nine feet tall. He appeared as the sleepwalking Sir Waltzworthy in the madcap play *Nighty Knight* over two thousand times. He is famous for finding surprising ways to make his stage entrances.

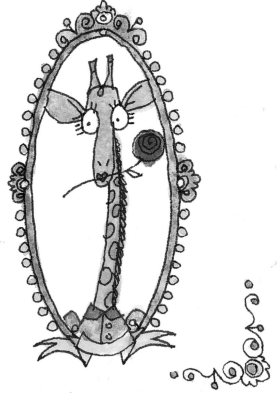

DAFFODIL CHANDELIER is renowned for dancing the complete bug ballet repertoire. She has dazzled audiences in *Lit by Fireflies*, *The Loveliest Ladybug*, *Flight of the Butterfly*, *The Mosquito Waltz*, and *A Moth in a Moonbeam*. She is the star pupil of legendary dance instructor Madame Flora Cavalletta.

To my brother,
Stephen, who
deserves a standing
ovation —V.X.K.

Copyright © 2012 by Vincent X. Kirsch
All rights reserved
Distributed in Canada by D&M Publishers, Inc.
Color separations by KHL Chroma Graphics
Printed in China by South China Printing Co. Ltd.,
Dongguan City, Guangdong Province
Designed by Roberta Pressel
First edition, 2012
1   3   5   7   9   10   8   6   4   2

mackids.com

Library of Congress Cataloging-in-Publication Data
Kirsch, Vincent X.
    The Chandeliers / Vincent X. Kirsch. – 1st ed.
        p.   cm.
    Summary: Night after night, Rufus Chandelier watches his family of
highly talented giraffes put on the greatest show in town, longing to
be big enough to join them, until he finally gets his chance to perform.
    ISBN: 978-0-374-39898-9
    [1. Revues–Fiction.   2. Giraffes–Fiction.   3. Humorous stories.]   I. Title.

PZ7.K6383Ch 2012   2013
[E]–dc22   Z0082447
                                            2010022314

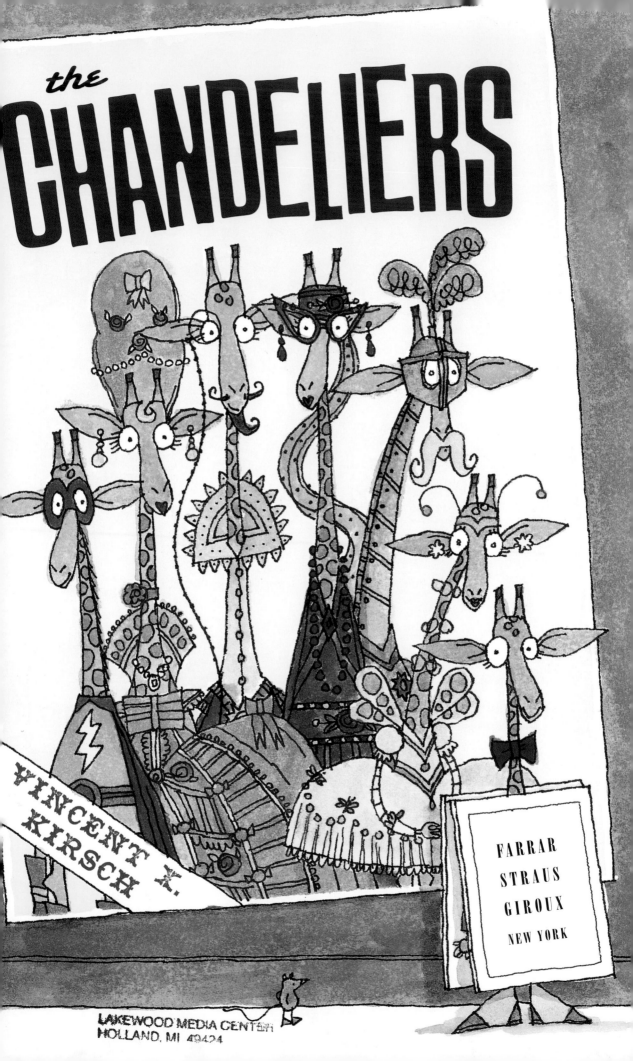

the CHANDELIERS

VINCENT X. KIRSCH

FARRAR
STRAUS
GIROUX
NEW YORK

MAXIMILIAN   DAPHNE   GRANDDADDY

Night after night, the Chandelier family put on the greatest show in town. Little Rufus Chandelier was not big enough to perform in the show, but he would stay up late and watch it. Until one night . . .

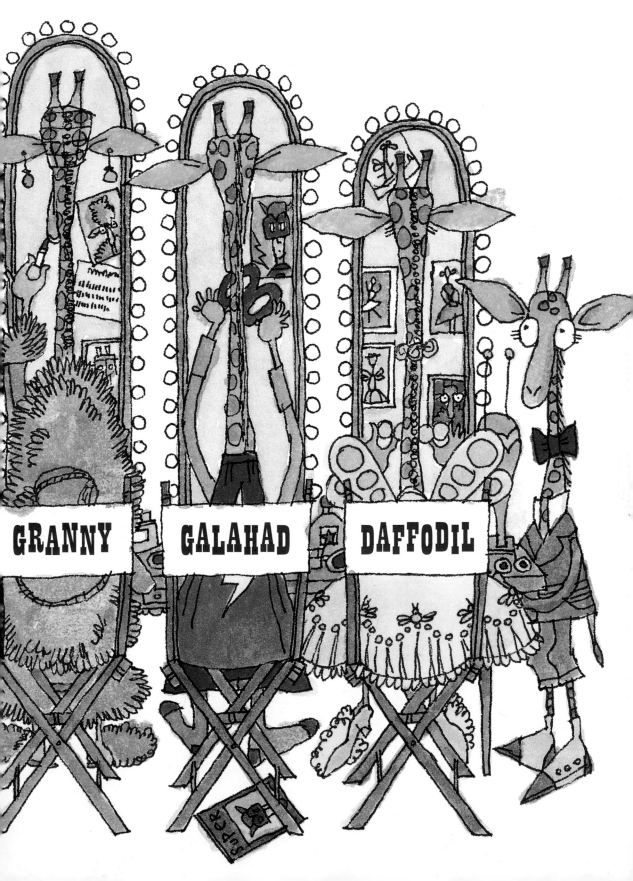

GRANNY   GALAHAD   DAFFODIL

Granny Chandelier almost
made her entrance with her
dress and wig on backwards.
Rufus straightened her out.

When it was time for Mr. Maximilian Chandelier's big speech, he could not remember what he was supposed to say. Rufus reminded him.

Mrs. Daphne Chandelier
hurried onstage without her
parasol. Rufus brought it
to her.

Granddaddy Chandelier got
stuck in the trapdoor. Rufus
helped him get through.

Daffodil Chandelier danced her famous bumblebee ballet. Rufus conducted the bumblebee band.

Galahad Chandelier galloped in on horseback.

Rufus galloped in right behind.

To add some suspense to the show, the Chandeliers wondered, "Hark! Is that thunder we hear?" There wasn't any thunder until Rufus made some.

For a little mystery, the Chandeliers exclaimed, "Look yonder! A full moon means there is danger afoot!" Rufus saw to it that there was a full moon.

The Chandeliers appeared to be in great danger.
Rufus made it appear very dangerous indeed.

The Chandeliers had to make a quick escape.
Rufus pedaled.

The Chandeliers did not get very far. They knew that the audience was expecting a happy ending. A cheerful song accompanied by a tuba did the trick.

But before the Chandeliers could finish their song, all at once the lights went out. Rufus quickly figured out how to switch them back on.

The Chandeliers took their bows.

Rufus gathered the flowers.

The Chandeliers took more bows. Rufus gathered more flowers.

That night, Mr. Maximilian Chandelier made a special announcement: "We are delighted that you liked the greatest show in town. But alas, we could not have done it without the wonderful Rufus Chandelier!"

And that night, Rufus got to take a bow.